For my
grandson
Tom Brown

This paperback edition first published in 2018 by Andersen Press Ltd.

First published in Great Britain in 2015 by Andersen Press Ltd.,

20 Vauxhall Bridge Road, London SW1V 2SA.

Copyright © Ruth Brown, 2015.

The right of Ruth Brown to be identified

as the author and illustrator of this work has

been asserted by her in accordance with the

Copyright, Designs and Patents Act, 1988.

All rights reserved.

Colour separated in Switzerland by Photolitho AG, Zürich.

Printed and bound in Malaysia.

2   4   6   8   10   9   7   5   3   1

British Library Cataloguing in Publication Data available.

ISBN 978 1 78344 216 4

FOREWORD

Anna Sewell said she wrote
Black Beauty "to induce kindness, sympathy
and an understanding treatment of horses".
It was the first book written from the point
of view of a horse and it was an immediate
success. As a direct result of her portrayal of
the harsh treatment of animals, Anna
Sewell not only improved the lives of
carriage horses, but of all other
working animals too.

Anna Sewell's
Black Beauty

Retold and illustrated by
Ruth Brown

ANDERSEN PRESS

Life was good on the farm where
I was born. The sun shone and
the grass was sweet.

I was jet black like my mother, but with a star on my forehead, one white foot and a small patch of white hair on my back. Mother taught me that although it was important to be obedient, it was more important to trust my own instincts.

When I grew up I went to work at a grand house as one of their carriage
horses. Life there was different, but the people were nice and so were
the horses, especially one called Ginger. She became my best friend.

Dear, nervous Ginger. She trusted no one. Then, one terrible night, a fire broke out in our stables. As flames roared through the yard, I instinctively let the groom lead me to safety. But Ginger wouldn't leave her stall. I called out to her that I was safe and that she would be too. Finally, she let the groom lead her safely through the smoke.

I saved my master too, one stormy night. As we drove
towards a bridge I stopped and refused to move –
I instinctively knew it was not safe to cross. And I was right.
When he shone his lantern, my master saw that the swollen
river had washed half the bridge away.

My reward was a special
supper brought by Joe Green,
our kindly new groom. Later, Joe nearly
killed me with kindness. But it wasn't his fault. He
didn't know that after a gallop he should cover me with a blanket.
Instead he gave me a huge bucket of water to drink, which upset
my stomach. I got a fever and Joe got into trouble. Luckily I soon
recovered and Joe had learnt his lesson.

Our master decided to move abroad, but fortunately Ginger and I were sold together. Our new groom was not as kind as Joe and he was careless. One night he rode me at a gallop over rough ground, though he knew one of my shoes was loose. When the shoe came off a sharp stone pierced my hoof. I stumbled and fell, throwing him over a hedge.

The pain from my hoof and cut knees was so bad, I couldn't go on. I waited for hours in the silent night until, eventually, I heard voices and the sound of hooves. I cried out and was overjoyed to hear Ginger's answering call.

While my wounds healed, I was put in the meadow.
When Ginger joined me, I was as happy as I had been
with my mother all those years ago. But our time
together was short. Only perfect horses were allowed
to pull our master's carriages. Because of my badly
scarred knees, I was no longer considered perfect and
so I was sold. I never saw Ginger again.

Over the next few years I passed from
one master to another. I felt miserable and missed
Ginger. Finally a kind London cabby called Jerry Baker
bought me and I knew life would be better. We worked hard,
especially at Christmas time. Waiting in the freezing night air
to take the party-goers home eventually made poor Jerry ill.
He had to give up work and that meant he had to give me up too.

My new owner, Mr Skinner, was mean. He put me in
a filthy stable and made me carry horribly heavy loads.
One day I crashed to the ground and couldn't get up.
I had had enough. Skinner wanted rid of me, but his
stableman said that with rest I'd fetch more money.

At the horse sale, as I joined the line of broken-down old horses, I saw a kind-looking farmer and lad looking at me. The boy begged his grandpa to buy me, so I held my head high and hoped for the best.

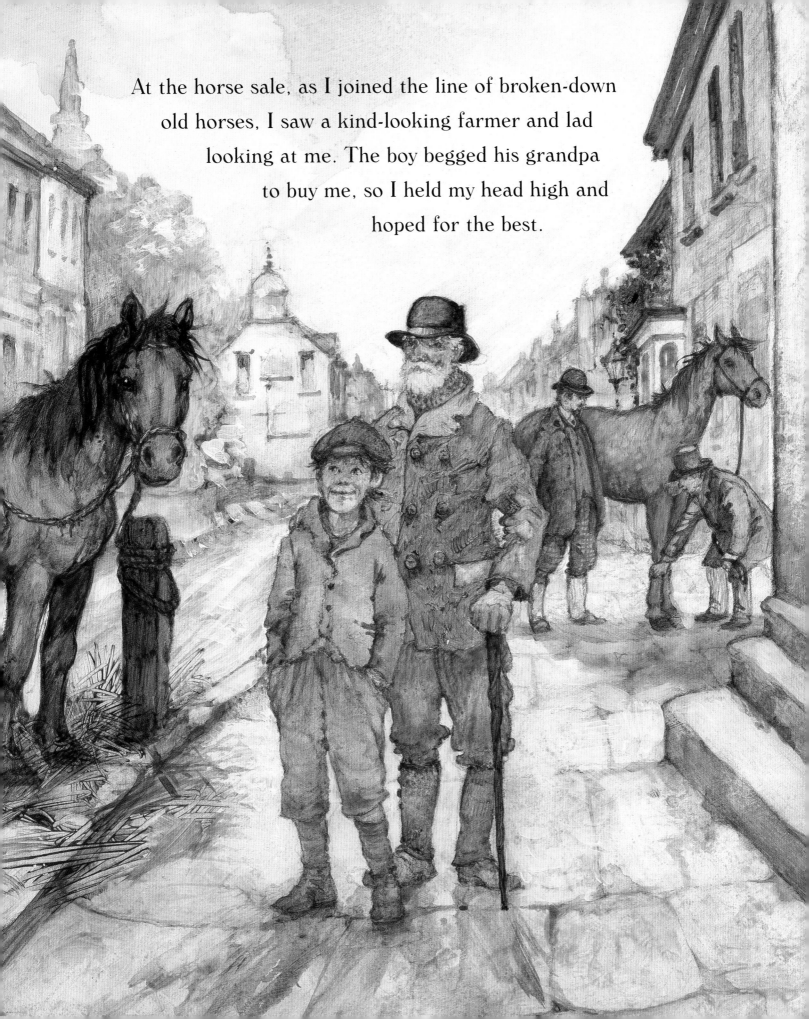

Once again my instincts were right – Willie and his grandpa were as good and kind as could be. Willie brought me oats every day and by spring I was feeling much better. Grandpa said that three gentle ladies who lived close by needed a good-tempered horse and would like to try me out.

As their groom led me
towards the stables, he stopped.
He stroked the star on my forehead,
examined my white foot, then gently ran his hand
along my back and found the patch of white hair.
"Black Beauty!" he cried "It IS you."
He laughed and hugged my neck.

"Don't you recognise me? I'm Joe Green – older
and wise enough now to look after you properly.
Try-out indeed! There's no more gentle horse
in the world than my Black Beauty."

Dear, kind Joe.
I knew then that
my troubles
were over. I
was home at
last and life
was good.

ABOUT THE AUTHOR

Anna Sewell was born in 1820 in Great
Yarmouth. Disabled by a childhood accident,
she relied on horse-drawn carriages and this
gave her a life-long love of horses. In 1871,
housebound and with her health declining,
Anna started to put this respect and concern
for the welfare of animals into words.
Her book, *Black Beauty*, was published
in 1877. She lived just long
enough to enjoy its success.
She died in 1878.